Cover Photograph
By
Karla Wolfson

*To All The Little
Tadpoles Who Will
Grow Up To Be
Beautiful Frogs.*

FROGDOGGY

JOAN FIELDING

Dear Readers,

Please let me know if you enjoy my story by emailing me at
joanfielding@comcast.net

To order additional copies of this book, contact:
Bookwhip
1-855-339-3589
https://www.bookwhip.com

The little frog sat on a lily pad night after night and stared through the big window of the house by the pond.

Let me tell you about Froggy: he wouldn't eat bugs like the other frogs in the pond. He caught them and pretended to eat them because he didn't want the other frogs to think he was a sissy. He was just… DIFFERENT!

Why oh why am I a frog, he thought to himself. I don't feel like a frog…I feel like a dog…I WANT TO BE A DOG!

Every night Froggy watched through the window where mother, father and a little girl sat in front of a cozy warm fireplace, talking and laughing and reading wonderful stories. Oh how he wanted to be a little dog sitting there with them. If he closed his eyes, he could pretend he was really there.

Finally, one moonlit night, he could not wait one minute longer.
He hopped off his lily pad and right up to the big window to get a
closer look; while he watched a big tear rolled down his cheek.

A Dragon Fly flew by, noticed the tear and ever so gently hovered
and asked. "What's the matter froggy, why are you so sad?" The little
frog said "n-n-nothings the matter."

"Well," said Flossy Dragon Fly, "Something is wrong! Froggy, some times you just can't wait for things to happen.

Sometimes you have to get going and make things happen yourself.

Froggy hopped slowly back to his familiar lilly pad. He felt just like he was in jail, but he really didn't understand why.

Then Froggy heard something and as he watched, a big truck drove up the driveway. A man got out of the truck with a package and walked right up to the front door and knocked on it.

Froggy watched as the little girl's father got out of his chair and walked to the door and opened it. The delivery man followed the father into the house with the package leaving the door open, just a little, but just far enough for a little frog to sneak inside.

This was Froggy's big chance. Ever so quietly he hopped into the room and hid behind the leg of a chair. Froggy sat ever so still and was almost afraid to breathe in fear someone would see him. He had come so far from his lily pad...he couldn't stop now.

Each day Froggy was in the house, he got a little braver but he was afraid the little girl (he heard her Mother call her Cassie) would see him and be afraid, or even worse, see him and hate just the sight of him.

FINALLY, when he couldn't stand it one minute longer; Froggy took a big gulp and a great big hop, and he jumped right in Cassie's lap. He closed his eyes, and he didn't care about anything else but being there, if only for a minute.

THEN IT HAPPENED! Cassie touched him gently on his head and said, "Hello, who are you"? "What's your name?" Froggy gulped...and gulped again, "I-I'm a DOG and my name is Spot," Froggy said. As soon as said it, he could hear his Mother say:

"Never, ever tell a lie, because you'll be very, very sorry if you do".

"Oh" said Cassie. I've always wanted a dog. Look Mommy, look Daddy, I have a little dog for my very own."

Cassie's mother jumped up very startled and started to brush the frog from Cassie's lap but Cassie's father stopped her and said, "Look Mother, at the little dog that has jumped in Cassie's lap. It is making her so happy." Mother looked at Cassie and saw that indeed, Cassie was happier than ever before so Mother sat back down.

Every night the little family would sit in front of the fireplace and enjoy just being with each other. Father had a beautiful voice and would sing beautiful songs. Sometimes Mother and Cassie would sing along. Froggy never, ever sang along (he was afraid he would croak like a frog), but even if he couldn't sing along, Froggy was very happy now that he was a dog. It was just like he knew it would be.

One morning a letter came in the mail that made Mother and Father very excited.

The very next day, Mother, Father, and Cassie drove off in their big car. When they came home, Cassie had a big bandage over her eyes and it had to stay on until the next day.

Froggy was so worried...for Cassie and for himself! He heard Mother and Father talking about the doctor they had seen and that Cassie had been blind since she was a baby and that by tomorrow maybe she would be able to see again.

Froggy doesn't know what to do. He only wants what's best for Cassie because he loves her so much but he knows if she can see she will know he lied and he is not really a dog named Spot...only a little frog with warts. He knows he deserves it too — for telling Cassie a big fat lie.

Froggy's mother was right. He should have listened and never told a lie . . .No matter what!

The next day, the doctor came and took the bandages off Cassie's eyes as Froggy watched from behind the chair where he had spent so many happy hours.

Cassie COULD SEE! She wasn't blind any more.

After all the kisses, hugs, tears and laughter were at last finally over, Froggy, with two big tears running down his cheek, started hopping to the front door.

He's going to sneak out with the doctor when the doctor leaves and return to his lilly pad in the pond so Cassie won't have to see him.

Before he could make his get-a-way and to his surprise, Cassie sat down by Froggy and said, "Don't cry Spot, It's all right. I love you just the way you are, warts and all.

Even when I was blind, my heart could still see. I knew all along you were a frog but you'll always be a dog to me."

So, always remember the story of Froggy and Cassie, No matter how you look on the outside, whether you think you are too short or too tall; too fat or too skinny, too loud or too shy or anything else you think is wrong with you--it doesn't matter.

There is only one person in the whole wide world who is You!

THAT MAKES YOU VERY SPECIAL.

Most of all remember, UNLIKE THIS BOUQUET OF FLOWERS, you can't tell about a person from the way they look on the outside...you have to look at the heart that's inside. That is where the love is.

Joan Fielding

A Freelance Illistrator/graphic Designer and Consultant, Joan graduated high school with a scholarship to the Chicago Art Institute. After her introduction to Sarasota with a successful art presentation at The American Bank of Sarasota, she launched Fielding Design Studio, a public relations marketing firm.

Joan is especially proud and credited for creating the concept design and marketing campaign, providing all original graphics and copy, for Breast Health Sarasota, Inc., sponsored by Sarasota Ford, Sarasota Memorial Hospital and The Sarasota Herald Tribune. Recognized nationally, BHS was absorbed by The Susan G. Komen Breast Health Organization.

Joan also served as Art Director for Sarasota Sailor Circus through the celebration of its' 50th Anniversary. Joan designes yearly manuals for Sarasota County and many entertainment industry clients.   She is an accomplished Illustrator of children's books and has recently published her first novel for adult audiences, *"LIVE LARGE FALL HARD."*

Joan is proud to be a Commissioned Kentucky Colonel for her service and accomplishments on behalf of her fellow man.

Joan's motto is:
"It's Nice To Be Nice"

A huge thank you to my incredible readers for all the emails they have
taken the time to send me. You are my inspiration, and as long as you keep reading and
enjoying my books, I will keep writing.

The following pages showcase
more titles by Joan Fielding also available on Amazon

BIG BAD RED

One last kiss good-bye for Mom before Penny and I leave for a fun summer with Aunt Becky in the Beautiful Tennessee Smoky Mountains. We will meet new friends and enjoy our nountain home until Mom finds a new home in Florida and comes for us. We are arriving with a surprise! My mate, Penny, has our baby in her pouch.

BY JOAN FIELDING

This story is about Luck, Love and Learning. What would you do if you won Six Million Dollars in the Florida Lottery?

Through the pages in this book, you will experience how life's journey can take you to places you wouldn't dare dream about if you could even imagine they exist.

Never stop dreaming and believing in miracles, because they do exist. I am living proof that happy endings are sometimes just around the corner.

More and more you see Kangaroos and Wallabys being sold as pets in the U.S.A. and it worries me. I intend to devote my life to make sure there is no unwanted pet Kangaroo or Wallaby without a home, food, water and most of all, love.

LOGAN
Fielding
ILLUSTRATIONS AND STORY by JOAN FIELDING

This Is an exciting adventure story about Logan, who receives help from a Firefighter / First Responder named Tim when he refuses to go to school and won't say why.

Through the pages in this book, your child will learn some of life's most important lessons while being totally entertained and completely engrossed in the story about a boy just like him.

There are bullies to get the best of and a big storm with thunder and lightening which provides an exciting reading experience leading to a very surprising ending.

THE ADVENTURES OF WISSY-WIG

WHO WILL BE CHOSEN???

**The citizen's of Planet Perfuma are desperate; they must find someone
brave enough to travel through the whole Galaxy,
find Planet Earth and ask for help or they are doomed.**

Long ago Planet Perfuma's Forefathers found a way to turn garbage into fuel. Perfuma is now running out of garbage.

Wissywig (WISSY-WIG) is the one who is chosen to save Planet Perfuma. **GIGO** is the name of Wysiwyg's spaceship. It means "Garbage In Garbage Out."

(WISSY-WIG) travels through the Galaxy searching for Planet Earth, he enjoys a drink of milk from the Big Dipper; slides down a rainbow and almost falls head first into the Pot Of Gold. (Plus other fun Galatic adventures)

(WISSY-WIG) visits the Statue of Liberty in New York City. (Educational)

When Wysiwyg arrives at the White House, the President's dogs bark and alert the Secret Service.

The Presdent stops the guards from shooting Wysiwyg down just in time.

The removal of all the garbage on Earth solves the problem of Greenhouse Gas and Global Warming.

Our first adventure ends as Wysiwyg and the President are honored as heroes for saving both Planet Earth and also Planet Perfuma.

(WISSY-WIG) is sure that he will travel through the galaxy again. Where ever he can be of service, he and his faithful space craft GIGO will be there to help.

(WISSY-WIG)
No. 1   The
Adventures of
Wysiwyg
Pronounced Wissy-Wig
Story and Graphics
By Joan Fielding
WOOOOOOSH
NEW YORK City

Dear Momsy,

I looked out my window and just saw the tiniest, the littlest, baby green froggy I ever saw in my life… It was a messenger of sorts, I am pretty sure of that.

I caught the little guy in a piece of (clean) toilet paper and gently placed him outside. While he was in my hand I said a little prayer, I said: "Little Froggy, I have done some terrible things in my life (according to my inner rules of ethics), I have said some mean things . . some I meant and some I didn't. But, one thing I would never do intentionally is hurt my mommy'a feelings.

So, little Froggie, if you are a little messenger . . . I am gently placing you outside in this grand, big big BIG place we call Planet Earth and asking you to hop along your Life's path and find my wonderful Mom…. I call her Heaven Sent (usually she answers to Momsy), and when you find her being that you are the messenger, Little Froggy. . Tell her that her I love her sooo much….

I want you to relay this message to my Mother. That she is wonderful and I wouldn't change a single hair on her beautiful head, but, most of all, little froggy make sure to tell her I would never mean to hurt her feelings in truth or in jest… her feelings are important to me and I would not hurt her for all the money or garbage in this world !

Tell her to forgive me for all my shortcomings (it is not my fault I am still learning) but if an apology is ever due make sure that you hand her that little card I gave you that said, "I'm sorry Momsy, I don't ever want to, or mean to hurt your feelings".

Froggy, you found your place in Life. You are a perfectly wonderful little shiny green messenger. Now, hop to it and deliver my message to my Mother. And say Goodnight, Sweet Dreams.

Time has a way of healing but the memories linger, so be careful little froggy on your Life's journey, surely you too will stumble your cute little froggy toes and hopefully you will be fortunate enough that you will be forgiven too. Hop along, Hop along hand in hand we go !

Love. Tadpole #2